·SPINKY·SULKS·

WILLIAM STEIG

A TRUMPET CLUB SPECIAL EDITION

To Jonathan, Alicia, Sido, Estelle, Jonas, Kyle, and Serena

Published by The Trumpet Club
666 Fifth Avenue, New York, New York 10103

Copyright © 1988 by William Steig
All rights reserved.

ISBN: 0-440-84352-9

This edition published by arrangement with
Michael di Capua Books/Farrar, Straus and Giroux
Designed by Atha Tehon
Printed in the United States of America
October 1990

10 9 8 7 6 5 4 3 2 1
UPC

Spinky came charging out of the house and flung himself on the grass. He couldn't even see the dandelions he was staring at, he was so upset. His stupid family! They were supposed to love him, but the heck they did. Not even his mother.

In a while his sister, Willamina, came out and said, "I'm sorry I called you Stinky, Spinky." Spinky didn't answer.

"Spinkalink," she said. "I apologize!" Spinky still didn't answer, so she went back inside. "*Now* she apologizes," he muttered.

A little later Spinky's brother, Hitch, appeared and touched him with a finger. Spinky shook it off. "You were posilutely right!" Hitch said. "I looked it up. Philadelphia *is* the capital of Belgium."

Spinky turned his back. His brother's slimy voice was more than he could bear.

"Spinks, it's lunchtime," said Hitch. "Mama wants you in the house."

Instead of answering, Spinky went and climbed the big tree.

His parents were watching from the window. "Poor kid, he's so sensitive," said his mother. "I better go talk to him, Harry."

"Ruby, don't," his father said. "He needs to simmer down. He's got no reason to sulk."

When it started getting dark, Spinky's mother came outside. She kissed him over and over, and told him she loved him with all her heart, ever since the minute he was born. And even before that.

Then she covered him with a blanket and kissed him again—and it was no fake kiss. But Spinky lay there like a stone. He wasn't interested in kisses that came too late.

The next morning, when Spinky's father left for work, Spinky was nowhere in sight.

Two seconds later he was in back of the house kicking a kerosene can. "Some father!" he snorted.

At noon Spinky's mother brought him a tray. Spinky didn't even look at her. "All of a sudden they're being nice!" he thought.

When she came back, the tomato soup and the asparagus were still there, but the crullers and the grapes were gone.

Hitch and Willamina kept finding Spinky in different places.

They'd try to pry a word out of him, or they'd just pass him by.

Hitch got down on his ugly knees once and begged to be forgiven
for anything he had ever done that Spinky took exception to. This only
made Spinky loathe him all the more.

Spinky's mother sat with him and held his hand, but his arm hung down like a noodle.

Willamina picked some daisies and stuck them in the hammock. Spinky threw them out.

Around four o'clock, a circus parade came marching by. "Look, Spinky," his mother cried. "Clowns! Elephants!" But he wouldn't even glance in that direction.

What a family! First they ruin his life, then they expect him to watch
a parade.

Spinky's best buddies, Smudge and Iggie, came to visit. Smudge crawled into the hammock and whispered goofy things in Spinky's ear. Spinky kicked him out.

Smudge and Iggie tried swinging him. Spinky usually liked that, but not now. He wrapped himself up in the hammock and disappeared, so his friends took off.

That evening Spinky's father gave him a long lecture. He said even though Spinky was wrong to sulk like a baby, everyone still loved him anyway. In fact, maybe he didn't realize it, but he was one of the most popular of the three children.

Spinky had to cover his ears to avoid listening to this malarky. No one seemed to understand that he was a person with his own private thoughts and feelings, which they couldn't begin to appreciate. The world was against him, so he was against the world, and that included all living things—except, of course, the animals.

Spinky's family was worried. They couldn't stand to see him feeling so wretched. That night they had a conference, and Spinky's father made a couple of phone calls.

The next day was a holiday. The sun was radiant, the birds were happy. Spinky couldn't care less. He lay in his hammock like a pile of laundry.

His favorite grandma just happened to stop by with some of his favorite candy. She gave him a big fat hug, but Spinky went limp in her arms.

After all, she still belonged to the human race, for which he no longer had any use.

Just then a circus clown happened to come prancing across the lawn with a sign saying: WE LOVE YOU, SPINKY. The clown winked, reached into Spinky's pocket, and pulled out a triple-dip ice-cream cone (pistachio, banana, and chocolate chip).

Spinky had to laugh. But then he saw his father smirking—and got the picture. The clown had been *hired* to cheer him up. Well, it wouldn't work!

All day long, everybody was as sweet and considerate as they could possibly be. When it started to rain, Spinky's mother covered him with a tarpaulin and his father set up the beach umbrella.

Hitch and Willamina served him cake and sandwiches. Still, Spinky couldn't give in, though he was beginning to consider it.

Maybe these people didn't know how to behave, but at least they were trying. Was it their fault they couldn't do better? He wasn't mad anymore, but he still had his pride. After all his suffering, how could he just turn around and act lovey-dovey? That wasn't his way.

Spinky lay awake wondering how to give in and still keep his self-respect. He decided he would take them by surprise.

Before dawn, he stole into the house and tiptoed about, very busy with secret business.

In the morning, the whole family drifted down to the dining room in a dreary mood. Laid out before them was a splendiferous feast, and there stood a garish clown, inviting them to join him.

Of course, they knew who it was. They laughed so hard it was
a long time before they could stop.

After that, Spinky's family was much more careful about his feelings.

Too bad they couldn't keep it up forever.